A Whitman TWEEN-AGE Book

In-between books for in-between readers.

ADVENTURES WITH HAL

ABOUT THIS BOOK

First take Grandpa Gale, who knows all about camping and the out-of-doors . . .

Then take Grandma Gale, who is about the best cook in the whole Northwest . . .

And don't forget a friendly spaniel named Hero . . .

Look around for a lake with fish to catch, bordered by woods just filled with interesting tracks, trails, and animals—including *bears!*

Add Hal Gale and his four lively cousins, Polly, Katie, Scotty, and Rex, all from different parts of the country, all with lots of enthusiasm and curiosity. And what have you got? Why, you've got a book packed full of good times and excitement—ADVENTURES WITH HAL.

Adventures with Hal

by Gladys Baker Bond

illustrated by
Polly Bolian

WHITMAN PUBLISHING COMPANY • Racine, Wisconsin

Library of Congress Catalog Card Number: 65-21125

© Copyright 1965 by Western Publishing Company, Inc.
WHITMAN PUBLISHING COMPANY
RACINE, WISCONSIN

Printed in the U.S.A. by Western Printing and Lithographing Company

CONTENTS

HAL'S SPECIAL DAY

"This is the day," Dad said when he loaded the car.

When the Gales passed the city limits Mother said, "The Day!"

"Oh, yes. THE DAY!" Hal echoed. His grin was so wide it wiggled his cheeks.

The day meant that Hal was on his way to visit Grandpa and Grandma Gale. They were now at their summer cottage on Blue Lake. By noon Hal would be out of the Snake River valley. He would cross the Washington wheatlands and enter the lake country of Idaho. After the weekend Mother and Dad would go back to the city.

"And," Hal thought happily, "that leaves just Grandma and Grandpa and me. Nobody else. Oh-h, boy. Maybe this year Grandpa will take me camping."

When Dad was Hal's age there had been no cottage on Blue Lake. When summer came Grandpa, Grandma, and their five sons had lived in a tent on a cliff. Whole families of deer played tag on the beach in the moonlight. Beavers built a dam in the creek. Bears roamed the woods. Coyotes hunted at night. A cougar, a great forest cat, mostly slept through the summer heat. But it liked the big, smooth cliff stones.

All his life Hal had heard the stories of Dad's childhood. But hearing was not enough. Hal wanted to *live* an adventure!

Grandpa had promised, "When you're old enough, and big enough, and smart enough, I'll take you camping. *That* will be an *adventure!*"

12

Of two things, Hal was sure. At ten, he was old enough. He was big enough. His head now reached Grandpa's shoulders. Grandpa was not a big man, but he "stood tall."

But, smart enough? Mm-m-m. Hal wondered about that part of Grandpa's promise.

Grandpa had been born on a ranch. He had raised his sons in logging camps. Grandpa knew woods, rivers, lakes, and animals. He knew it takes more than courage to live safely in the wilderness.

"Takes know-how, boy," was Grandpa's explanation.

Hal lived in a city in the treeless wheatlands. What he knew about the forest he had learned by visits with Grandpa and through reading.

Hal had read every nature book on the reading table in his schoolroom. He had joined Cub Scouts. First he was a Bobcat, then a Wolf. Now he was ready for the Bear trail. Would Grandpa think he was smart enough to go camping?

Just thinking about it made Hal slide to the edge of the backseat. Anxiously he looked through a window. Were they almost at Blue Lake? No. All

he saw was a small ranch belonging to an Indian.

"Can't you drive faster, Dad?" Hal urged.

"Want me to get arrested for speeding?" Dad asked.

Dad winked at Mother, but he did not drive faster. So Hal's brain buzzed like a hive of bees while he planned his summer with Grandpa and Grandma. Grandpa liked the things Hal liked: apple pie, hot sun, the tug of a fish on his line, exploring, dogs, and boys. Hal was especially glad Grandpa liked boys.

Hal thought about reaching the lake. Grandpa would be waiting at the mailbox on the County Road. Grandpa's spaniel, Hero, would hear the car. He would race to meet it. Grandpa and Hero would ride down the lane in the backseat with Hal. They would talk about fishing, hiking, swimming, and beach fires. And, oh, Grandma was the best cook in Idaho. The lunch she prepared would be a dinner.

"If we don't get there pretty soon, I'll—I'll pop!" Hal told Dad.

Dad chuckled. "I'll deliver you to Grandpa in one piece," he teased. "Here is the golf course."

Hal knew how many curves were in the road from the greens to the cottage. He began to count. "One! Two! Three!" When he shouted, "Sixteen!" he sat on the edge of the backseat and looked down the lane.

Dad honked the horn. Mother rolled down a window, ready to wave and shout.

There stood the mailbox with Grandpa's name on it. But Grandpa was not sitting in the shade. Hero did not run to meet the car.

"Where's Grandpa?" Hal asked.

"Maybe he's busy," Dad said.

Dad drove slowly down the lane. They did not meet Grandpa.

When they reached the parking lot, Grandpa was not in sight. Nor was Hero.

But—the parking lot was full of cars: red, blue, white, and yellow. Puzzled, Hal read the license plates aloud. "New York, Missouri, Washington, Georgia. Who—"

"I know!" Dad shouted. He did not even stop to unload the car. He put the key in his pocket and ran as fast as his long legs would move. He did not stop

to open the gate, but jumped right over the fence.

Mother followed almost as fast, but she went through the gate.

Hal tried to keep up with Mother. He shouted, "Grandpa, I'm here!" And still Grandpa did not appear.

Several voices shouted, "Surprise, surprise, we're here, too!"

Up the path through the backyard raced two girls and two boys. The blond girl in the lead was Hal's cousin, Polly. But who was that girl with thick, brown braids? That boy with freckles? And that white, skinny boy with glasses?

They did not look like strangers. Still, Hal did not know them.

Dad knew them. He shouted, "Polly! Katie! Scott! Rex!"

Mother and Dad hugged the children. They rushed down the steep path to the cottage. Dad war whooped. Men's voices answered.

The minute Hal heard the names, he knew these girls and boys. They were his cousins!

Hal liked people. He wanted these four cousins

to like him—but, oh, would Grandpa take *five* children camping?

Quite openly Katie looked Hal up and down. Then she said, "Grandpa said you'd be brown as a cowboy, and you are. You look like my dad when he was a little boy."

"I'm not little," Hal said. He stood tall, but this Katie with the dark braids was taller.

"I know that," Katie said, giggling. "You're three months older than Rex, and he's ten. I'm eleven, and Scotty is nine, same as Polly."

The skinny boy with the glasses hitched up his belt. "I'm Rex," he said.

The freckled, plump boy grinned. He told Hal, "I'm Scotty."

Polly stepped out ahead of Rex, Katie, and Scotty. "Hal knows me," she said.

"We've been waiting for you, Hal," Katie chattered. "Grandpa says you will show us everything."

Rex pushed his glasses up on his nose. He said, "I live in New York City. Katie is from Kansas City, and Scotty lives in Savannah. When we get off a sidewalk, we're lost."

21

Hal swallowed. Oh, oh. Good-bye, camping trip!

Just when Hal's lips almost quivered, he looked at his cousins. Each cousin waited for a leader, and Grandpa had given him the job.

Inside Hal's head a voice said, "A Cub helps the pack go." Well, these cousins were now his pack. Hal made his lips smile. "L-Let's go!" he said.

The five cousins rushed down the path. They skidded on slippery pine needles. They shouted. Hal shouted loudest of all. If he made lots of noise he would not think about camping.

Grandpa walked around the corner of the cottage. While he waited, he bent his knees to ease their stiffness. A glad smile creased his cheeks. A breeze lifted his curly, white hair.

Hero pushed his nose into Grandpa's right hand. Then the spaniel raced up the path.

With a gay flip of the hand, Grandpa saluted Hal. "Hello, boy!" Grandpa said gladly. "Think you can help me get these city slickers ready for a camping trip in August?"

"Whillikers, yes, *sir!*" Hal whooped.

Then Hal saw a yardful of uncles and aunts. They

24

pulled him into the circle with Mother and Dad. The uncles said proudly, "Hal, you're a chip off the old block."

Cheerfully Grandpa asked, "Who's calling me an old block?"

A long table stood in the front yard. There were so many plates, Hal counted them. Seventeen!

Grandma came out of the cottage. She carried the biggest chocolate cake Hal had ever seen. She almost sang when she said, "Hello, Hal. Isn't this a wonderful day?"

Soon the Gale family gathered around the long table. Hal sat between Rex and Scotty. Hungrily he ate fried chicken, sliced tomatoes, and potato salad. He kept his eyes on Grandma's cake.

At the ends of the table Grandpa laughed and Grandma beamed. Dad and his brothers talked about Blue Lake before hundreds of people built cottages. Cousins and aunts chattered. Mother helped Grandma carry more food from the kitchen. Hero ran around and around the table.

Hal grinned till his cheeks wiggled. This was, indeed, a very special day.

HAL'S SECRET

Hal floated on his back and looked at the blue sky. It spread high, high above the tallest pines on the cliff. Above the beach Grandpa's cottage looked like a dollhouse on a shelf. On the shelf above it was the parking lot. Up on the ridge the mailboxes stood beside the County Road, but they were hidden by trees.

Grandpa and Scotty had walked up the hill for the mail. On the dock Polly was rubbing suntan oil on Katie's back. Rex practiced broad jumping on the sand. Grandma read under a red and yellow umbrella. It was such an ordinary day, Hal's camping trip seemed impossible.

26

Out in the bay a speedboat roared past. In a few seconds a wave rolled toward the beach. Water hit the top of Hal's head. It sloshed over his face. Hal rolled and sputtered. He sank to the sandy floor of the lake, then swam up to the surface.

When Hal's head rose out of the water, he found himself in the cool, secret room under the dock. Ten inches above the water, the dock floor made a ceiling. Dock logs formed walls. The floor was the sandy lake bottom.

A school of tiny fish darted out of the shadows. One swam through Hal's fingers. On a crossbar a fat frog blinked at Hal. Beetles crawled in moss.

Hal jumped when something slithered. Then he saw that it was not a snake. The movement was made by a long, flat black tail. The tail hung down from a tangle of weeds. Hal pulled in his breath. He had found a muskrat's summer nest!

The dock logs began to rock. When the water moved there was less space under the dock. Hal knew another speedboat had gone by. Afraid he might crack his head on a log, he swam out and up.

Just as he rose to the surface, he saw Grandpa

drop a number of letters on Grandma's lap.

On the dock Katie jumped up. Polly wailed, "You made me spill the suntan oil!"

Katie paid no attention to Polly. She shrieked, "Is there a letter for me, Grandpa?"

"Sorry, honey," Grandpa called back.

Both Rex and Scotty sat on the beach to read letters.

Hal saw the stiff way Katie stood, and the way her thin hands drew into fists.

Polly rescued the oil. She coaxed, "Sit down, Katie. I'll rub your back. I didn't get a letter either."

Katie choked out, "You didn't need one, Polly. Your mother called you on the phone. And Seattle isn't as far away as Kansas City!" She hugged herself to hide the trembling.

Hal had not paid much attention to this long-legged, nervous, talkative cousin with the thick, dark braids. Now he called, "Jump in, Katie. I'll show you my secret."

"Huh," Katie sniffed. "Wh-who wants to look at a fish?"

"Honest injun, it's not a fish," Hal said.

Polly offered eagerly, "I'll come, Hal."

Katie jumped up and scowled fiercely. "Hal asked *me*."

Katie did not know how to dive, but she tried. With a loud plop she landed flat on the water. Puffing, blowing, and churning water, she made her way to Hal. "Sh-show me," she gasped.

"Me, too?" Polly asked. Until Katie quit thrashing the water, Polly could not dive.

"Next," Hal promised. Polly sat down on her big beach towel. "We have to go under the dock," Hal told Katie.

"I can't swim underwater!" Katie argued.

"You don't have to," Hal said. "Just hold your nose. Hang onto me and I'll take you under."

Katie hesitated. Then she took a deep breath. She pinched her nose with one hand. With the other hand, she grabbed Hal's neck.

"I didn't say *drown* me!" Hal yelled.

Katie loosened her hold on his neck. She sank. Hal duck-dived and towed her under the dock. Katie splashed to the surface, still pinching her

30

nose. When she opened her eyes, she shrieked, "E-Eek!" She faced a big frog, eye to eye.

"Aw, he won't hurt you," Hal said. "See what I found. A muskrat."

"A rat?" Katie squealed. "Get me out of here!"

"A muskrat!" Hal corrected.

Just as Katie opened her mouth for another shriek, the long tail moved. A ball of dark brown fur backed out of the weeds. A small head appeared. The animal looked at them out of small, beady eyes and wiggled its nose. Three black feet moved. The fourth leg dangled.

"O-Oh," Katie crooned. "He's hurt, Hal."

Hal pulled himself along the dock logs. When he came near, the small animal shrank back. It bared its teeth.

"He thinks you're going to hurt him," Katie said softly.

Katie and Hal clung to a crossbar to watch the muskrat. After a while it humped its back and dozed.

"Do you suppose he's hungry?" Katie wondered.

"If he gets hungry enough, he'll eat his nest.

32

That's what they do in winter," Hal answered. "Muskrats feed at night. We'll come back after supper to see if he's still here."

Hal managed to pull Katie under the dock logs without drowning her. Then he shared his secret with Polly, Rex, and Scotty.

Polly found a knothole in the floor of the dock. Many times that day the cousins ran down to the dock to see the injured muskrat.

Not once did Katie mention having had no letter. She practiced dropping into the water and coming up in another spot. Hal stayed in the water to protect her.

Grandpa shouted from the cliff, "What on earth is Katie doing, bobbing around like a mud hen?"

"She wants to visit a sick friend," Hal called back. He ducked away from the water Katie splashed in his face.

That afternoon Katie received a letter. She read it aloud at the supper table.

Hal's place at the table faced the lake. Twice he saw muskrats swim toward the seaweed at the mouth of the creek. They left a long V-shaped wake in the water. Neither water trail left the dock.

Not one cousin lingered over Grandma's rice pudding. They rushed to the dock. Flat on stomachs, Rex, Scotty, Polly, and Hal lay in a row. They looked over the edge of the dock. The slit between the dock log and the dock floor allowed them to look at the muskrat. Katie peeped through the knothole.

"He's still there!" Katie said excitedly. "I know he's hungry."

After talking with Grandpa, the five cousins scattered to find water-lily roots, cattails, and swamp grass. They poked their offerings through the slit. The injured muskrat just humped his back.

Not even Hal asked to fish when the crappies began to jump. The cousins were worried about the muskrat. Just before bedtime they formed a flashlight parade and went to look at the little brown animal.

For two days the muskrat received their whole attention. They added seeds, roots, and leaves to their food offerings. The food wilted. The muskrat hunched on his platform of reeds and grass. His injured leg hung down.

"He'll starve," Katie worried. She was cleaning carrots for supper. She swished a feathery green top under Scotty's nose.

Plump, freckled Scotty always noticed odors. "Mmm," he said. "That top smells good enough to eat."

"Maybe—it—is," Katie said thoughtfully. She placed the carrots in a dish. Then she rushed from the kitchen.

At the dock Katie poked the carrot top through the knothole. Then she sat quietly, like a fisherman waiting for a bite. Hal and Polly waited with her. When Katie had almost given up, she felt a tug on the end of a carrot leaf. "Hal, he's eating!" Katie said. Her eyes widened with wonder. She was too happy to smile.

The next day the muskrat ate the bits of lettuce Polly poked through the knothole. Scotty fed it potato peelings. Rex offered a slice of apple on a stick.

"You haven't fed him, Hal," Katie said. "And you were the one who found him."

Grandpa said muskrats ate small water animals.

38

Hal had brought a ball of raw hamburger.

"I'm going to try something," he told Katie.

The cousins wore shorts and sneakers from morning till night. When Hal took off his sneakers, he was ready to swim. He slid into the water, careful not to splash, duck-dived, and came up under the dock.

The muskrat was eating Rex's apple. It paid little attention to Hal. Hal moved close. Carefully, oh, so carefully, he offered his hand. When he opened his fingers, the tiny ball of raw hamburger lay on his palm. Almost afraid to breathe, he waited.

The muskrat moved away, dragging its injured leg. Its nose twitched. Beady eyes studied Hal's hand. Cautiously the muskrat moved forward. When its nose caught the scent of Hal's fingers, its head jerked back. But hunger overcame fear. The muskrat ate the few crumbs of raw meat Hal offered.

Hal shivered with excitement. He had not been able to go to the wilderness, but a living part of the wilderness had come to him. A wild animal had eaten out of his hand. He must tell Katie. She would understand how he felt.

HAL UP A TREE

At the breakfast table, Grandma tapped her chin with one finger. She said, "If I had some apples, I'd bake an apple pie."

"Yummy!" Scotty said. Then he groaned. "Where'll we get apples?"

"I can find apples," Hal put in eagerly.

"My goodness, where?" Grandma asked.

"In the old orchard on the hill," Hal answered. "Above the County Road there is a farm. Nobody has lived there for a long time. Nobody picks the fruit in the orchard. I know we can find apples."

40

"Of course," Grandma agreed. "I'd forgotten about the old orchard."

Warily Polly asked, "How far is it?"

Polly was youngest of the cousins. Sometimes she found it hard to keep up with three boys and long-legged Katie. Also, Polly was plump and just a little bit lazy.

Hal burst out, "Polly, we will never get to go camping if you can't even walk up to the old orchard and back!" When Polly looked stubborn, Hal coaxed, "It isn't far. Honest, it isn't, Polly."

Polly held back. "I'd rather go swimming," she said.

Katie jiggled with impatience. "Come on, Polly. We can't swim for an hour after eating. By that time we'll be back at the cottage and ready to swim."

Polly looked doubtful, but she allowed herself to be coaxed.

"We won't walk too fast," Hal promised.

He ran for the pail Grandma kept under the sink.

"Wear your hats," Grandma reminded them. "It's hot on the hillside."

Wearing shirts and shorts, sneakers, and straw hats, the cousins left the cottage. Grandpa walked with them up the lane to the County Road.

Hal carried Grandma's pail. "But we have to take turns carrying home the apples," he insisted. "Good campers always share the work."

At the end of the lane Hero decided to stay with Grandpa. Grandpa left a letter in the mailbox, then started home. He called, "Stay on the road and you won't have a bit of trouble."

Beyond the end of the lane a grass-grown road led up the mountainside. Tree squirrels worked in the tops of the tallest pines. Chipmunks ran along fallen logs. Grasshoppers *clitter-clattered* in dry grass. A woodpecker tapped noisily on a dead fir tree. Once a pine snake slithered across the road. It slid into a hole under a stump.

Polly shrieked, "I'm going home!"

"Alone?" Hal asked, grinning.

Polly kicked at the grass between the road ruts. Rex, Scotty, and Katie walked on up the steep road.

"Wait for me!" Polly squealed.

44

"Well, hurry up, slowpoke," Hal answered. He was glad Grandpa was not here. He would never allow Polly to camp. If one couldn't go, none could go. Hal's chance of camping in August looked pretty dim.

By the time the cousins reached the farm, sun beat down on unmowed meadows and lonely buildings.

"Wow, is it ever hot!" Rex declared.

"Wish I'd brought the spring with me," Scotty said. He mopped his hot, freckled face.

Hal snapped his fingers. "I can find water," he said.

Swinging Grandma's pail, Hal led the way to a covered well. It was near the back door of the old farmhouse. A frayed rope remained on the reel of the pulley. Since there was no bucket, Hal tied the rope to Grandma's pail.

Rex and Scotty lifted the wooden well cover. Then Hal dropped the pail into the well. He reeled the rope onto the wooden spool to pull up the pail. As the pail of water began to rise, it seemed to grow heavier.

"Help me turn the crank, somebody," Hal begged. Willingly Rex placed his thin hands beside Hal's. Together they drew up the pail. Rex lifted it over the rim of the well. Water splashed when he set the pail in the thick grass.

After each cousin had drunk cold water, Rex noticed that the grass looked beaten down.

Scotty said, "It smells funny around here." When he sniffed, his freckles moved.

"Old houses always smell funny," Hal said.

Polly saw that Hal did not smile. Hal looked at the path.

The path led through tall, dry grass. Wire fences sagged. Fence posts leaned this way, that way. Grasshoppers, deerflies, and bees jumped and bit and buzzed. But insects had not made that path.

"You know something we don't know, Harold Gale," Polly accused.

Scotty started along the path. He beckoned. "Come on, I smell apples!" he shouted.

Rex asked, "Wh-what made this path? It smells just like the old house."

Hal remembered Grandpa had said you can find an animal if you know what it likes to eat. Well, Hal knew what liked to eat apples. Bears. "L-Let's go another way," he said shakily.

"It's easier to walk in the path," Katie argued.

Polly complained, "If we leave the path, we'll get scratched."

But in the end, both boys and girls followed Hal's

47

new path through the meadow to the orchard.

In the orchard the cousins hunted for the largest, juiciest apples. Katie climbed the tallest tree with Rex and Scotty. Polly chose a gnarled old tree which was easy to climb. Her tree stood beside the path to the farmhouse. Hal stayed on the ground.

Busily the cousins threw apples to Hal. He caught the fruit and put the apples in Grandma's pail.

Suddenly one of Polly's apples shot through the air. Hal jumped, but missed the apple. He shouted at Polly, "Grandma doesn't want bruised apples!"

"She doesn't want bruised boys, either!" Scotty yelled. "Climb, Hal!"

Quickly, Hal turned. He grabbed the first limb he could reach and swung up into the tree beside Polly.

For—there was a bear!

"It's—just—a c-cub," Polly stammered.

"Cubs have mothers," Hal answered.

The cub waddled up the path. It swung its head close to the ground. The bear's sharp nose touched the apple Polly had thrown. The bear raised its head. It squinted through small, piglike, nearsighted eyes.

48

"Oh, oh," Hal whispered. "He has our scent."

"Ugh," Polly choked. "We have his scent, too. What'll we do?"

Hal looked at Polly with respect. She shrieked at pine snakes and scratches. But she did not shed a tear when faced with a bear. Hal wished Grandpa could see Polly. He would say she was brave enough to camp.

But Hal was not so sure about his own courage. He could see that bear cub's claws.

Carefully Hal dropped an apple at the feet of the well-fed cub. The bear swung its head, then crunched hungrily. Hal saw Scotty's arm raised to throw an apple. Hal signaled the younger boy not to move. To Hal's relief, Rex, Scotty, and Katie understood his signal.

After a while Polly whispered, "I'm getting dizzy."

"Sh-h," Hal warned. "Don't look down."

"I have to keep my eyes on that bear," Polly insisted.

The five cousins clung to their apple-tree perches till even Hal thought he would have to move. And still that bear cub ate apples. Once the bear turned

50

as if to leave. It saw a line of ants leaving a hill. The cub clawed the anthill and licked up the ants.

Then the bear sat in the grass to scratch and stretch. Like a well-fed baby, the cub prepared to nap. It grumbled and whined. It did not find a comfortable bed in the grass. At last it waddled back through the orchard. From their high perches, the cousins saw it climb through a broken window of the old farmhouse.

"I'll bet he was *in* that house while we were at the well!" Rex burst out.

"That's what I smelled," Scotty said.

"Let's go home," Hal urged.

The five cousins scrambled out of the trees. Rex snatched up the pail of apples. Through the meadow they hurried, paying no attention to thistles. They reached the old road. Only then did they pause in the shade of some elderberry bushes.

Scotty grinned with relief. "We made it!" he said.

Katie pulled tree bark from her long braids. She asked, "Aren't grown-ups funny? Grandma told us to wear our hats. Grandpa told us to follow the road. But nobody warned us about bears!"

52

HERO'S FISH

After supper Polly and Katie won the race to the hammock in the front yard. So Hal, Rex, and Scotty lay on their stomachs in the cool grass. They flipped bits of pine cone at a white pebble.

Scotty kept track of hits and misses. But Hal kept track of Grandpa. Hal wanted to go fishing. Only Grandpa could give permission.

But Grandpa was not looking at the lake. He was listening to the news on his portable radio.

53

Loudly Hal said, "The fish are jumping!"

Just as Hal had hoped, Grandpa stood up. He looked out over Blue Lake.

Katie almost fell out of the hammock. She asked, "Where? Where?"

Hal pointed.

"Huh, I don't see a thing," Katie said.

"Katie, if you expect to go camping in August, you have to learn to see what's happening all around you," Hal argued.

Katie braced both hands on her hips. "How can I see, when there's nothing to see?" she asked.

Just then a fish rose from the water. It twisted into the air to catch an insect. Then it dropped back in a curving dive.

"See?" Hal told Katie.

Grandpa turned off his radio. He asked, "Hal, why don't you take the kids fishing?"

"All alone?" Hal wanted to fish, but he had never fished in the evening without Grandpa. Suddenly the lake looked almost as wide as an ocean. Shadows filled the valleys between the foothills. It looked lonesome down there on the beach.

But, a camp would be a long way back in the wilderness. Probably it would look lonesome, too. Lonesome or not, Hal wanted to be ready for that camping trip. He stuck out his chin and said, "Yes, sir!"

Grandpa winked and grinned. He said, "Crappies are good for breakfast."

Scotty jumped up. Eagerly he said, "If a crappie is something to eat, I'm ready to catch it."

"Me, too," Rex agreed.

56

The rack which held the fishing rods was on the wall near the hammock. As Grandpa walked toward the rack he asked, "Remember our rules, boy?"

Promptly Hal answered, "We're not to catch more than we need."

"And?" Grandpa asked.

Hal grinned slyly at Katie and Polly. "When we catch fish we must clean them," he said.

Polly said, "Ugh." She did not take a rod.

Carrying rods, Rex and Scotty started down the rocky path after Hal.

Katie looked uncertain. She followed the three boys all the way to the edge of the cliff. Then she decided she did not want to clean a fish. She went back to the yard to play hopscotch with Polly. Every few minutes Katie ran along the path to peer down on the lakeshore.

When the three boys reached the beach, Scotty and Rex raced down a long sandbar. "Dibs, dibs!" Scotty shouted. He wanted to stand at the very tip of the sandbar.

"You can't catch fish out there!" Hal yelled.

Scotty shouted cheerfully, "Why not? Fish swim in water. There's lots of water out here."

Hal called, "I'll show you the crappie hole. This way!" An echo bounced from the opposite cliff. An imp seemed to shout, "Hole . . . way!" Hal wondered if there would be an echo back in the wilderness. If so, he hoped it shouted only in the day-time.

Scotty and Rex ran down the sandbar. They followed Hal to his "crappie hole." At this spot a creek entered Blue Lake. Moving water dug a trench through sand. Mud had settled on the bottom. Seaweed grew under the water.

"When you know what fish and animals and birds eat and where they like to build their nests, you can find them," Hal explained.

Freckle-faced Scotty grinned. He teased, "I suppose the fish build a nest here."

"Yep," Hal said. "Right on the bottom."

"Honest?" Scotty asked in surprise.

Rex squinted through his thick glasses. "How?" he wanted to know.

"They swish a hole with their tails," Hal told the

60

boys. While he told them about nest building, Hal showed his cousins how to lengthen their rods. Then he showed them how the reel controls the line.

"Now, I'll cast," he said.

The fly hit the water with a dull plop. For just a minute Hal pretended he had made a perfect cast. Then he remembered he was supposed to be helping Grandpa train these boys for a camping trip. He grinned and said, "Oh, oh. I flubbed that one."

Hal tried again. This time his cast was almost as good as he wanted it to be.

A sunfish cut water. It took the fly and dived. With a snap of the wrist, Hal set the hook. He lifted his catch from the water. Rex and Scotty said, "Boy!" Their eyes were wide with admiration.

Sunset colors glowed on the fish's flat, silver-green body. Drops of water slid back into the lake. Rings spread out and out until broken by waves.

"So that's a crappie," Rex said.

"It's a kind of sunfish," Hal explained. He showed Rex and Scotty the crappie's short, wide body and notched tail. Then he put the fish on the fish stringer. Carefully he anchored the stringer in shallow water.

61

"We won't have a refrigerator back in the forest," he told his cousins.

Rex and Scotty chose fishing spots. Scotty's rod tip hit water. Rex's line dangled in the air.

"What are you trying to catch? Flying fish?" Hal teased. "Rex, let your fly float. Scotty, don't punch the water."

At just that moment Hal snagged another crappie. While he put it on the stringer, Scotty caught a fish. He yelled so loudly, Polly and Katie ran to the top of the cliff.

"Did you fall in, Scotty?" Katie shouted anxiously.

"Got one!" Scotty roared.

"Me, too!" Rex yelled.

The girls stayed at the top of the cliff to share the fun. The five cousins sang and shouted just to hear the echo throw back their words. In the cheerful uproar, Hal forgot to be lonesome.

After a while Grandpa and Grandma joined Katie and Polly. Hero raced down the cliff path. He bounced and barked each time a fish was caught.

He sniffed the fish on the stringer. Then Hero disappeared.

Sunset faded. Bats swooped in circles and fed on mosquitoes. One bat flew so close Hal heard its high-pitched squeak.

By the time the fish sank to the bottom for the night, the three boys had caught seven fish. As they climbed the cliff path, Scotty counted, "One each for Grandpa, Grandma, Katie, Polly, Rex, and Hal. Hey! Who gets the other fish?"

"Don't you want one?" Hal teased.

"Did I leave myself out?" Scotty asked cheerfully. "I want the biggest."

"Then you clean it," Hal told him just as cheerfully.

When they reached the top of the cliff Grandpa looked at the seven crappies on the fish stringer. "Good catch," he said.

Suddenly Hero raced up the path. He ran so fast his long ears flapped. In his mouth he carried a very large, very dead, and very smelly fish!

"You didn't catch a fish for Hero, so he caught his own," Grandpa said.

When Grandpa laughed, the echo laughed, too. Hal liked the sound.

HERO

Grandpa's spaniel, Hero, adopted the five cousins. All day long he ran till his feathery curls bounced. He kept track of each boy and girl. At night he padded through the house, clicking his toenails on the bare floor. At each cot he poked his cold nose against a hand or chin. Sometimes he jumped on the foot of a cot to sleep.

"Hero thinks he is people," Polly said. Hero wiggled and waggled to show he understood what she said.

But Hero did not understand being left out of anything. He sat in the boat when Grandpa fished. So he expected to sit in the boat when the cousins fished. But Grandpa said No.

66

One morning, long before breakfast, Grandpa, Hal, Rex, and Scotty left the cottage. They carried fishing tackle to the dock. Hero followed. He jumped into the boat before Grandpa unlocked the chain.

"No, Hero," Grandpa said. "Not this morning."

Hero jumped onto the dock. He cried and thumped the dock with his tail.

Hal begged, "Please, Grandpa? Hero doesn't take up much room."

"Neither does a fishhook," Grandpa answered dryly. "But I don't want a fishhook in Hero's nose."

"We'll be careful, Grandpa," Scotty promised. Rex was quietest of the cousins. But this morning even Rex coaxed.

Hero knew the boys wanted him. He rubbed against their legs. He made little talking sounds in his throat.

"No," Grandpa insisted. "Boys, dogs, fishhooks, and a boat don't mix well."

Hero ran circles on the dock. His nose pointed down. His tail drooped. He cried softly. Then when the boat pulled away from the dock, Hero sat down to wait.

"We'll be back soon," Hal promised the dog.

The boys watched Hero till he was a spot in the distance.

So early in the morning, trees on the ridges stuck up like the teeth of a gray comb. Fog floated just above the boat. Mud hens dived when the boat came near. Ducks rose. They dangled yellow legs. White sea gulls on logs moved uneasily when the boat passed.

When they reached deep water where the trout fed, Grandpa turned off the motor. Two boys rowed while one fished with Grandpa. This was their first chance to fish for trout. At the end of a long, long line a string of shiny lures held sharp hooks. It took skill to manage the troll line. Eagerly the boys did just what Grandpa said. They forgot about Hero.

Two rocky points stuck out into the bay on opposite sides of the lake. A wide stretch of open water lay between. Hal and Rex rowed from point to point. Then they circled and rowed back again, slowly. Grandpa whistled between his teeth. Scotty hummed. The oars squeaked. There was plenty of time to look at lake and shore.

68

As the sun rose above the foothills, the fog lifted. Far, far down the lake Hal could see Grandpa's cottage sitting on its rock shelf. When he squinted, Hal could see a dark spot. "Hero is waiting for us," he told Rex.

Rex wore thick glasses. When he took them off he could see twice as far as Hal could see. Now Rex pushed his glasses down on his nose. "Hero is watching us," Rex said.

Grandpa had a strike. "Steady with the oars. Don't let the boat swing," he told Hal and Rex.

By the time Grandpa had landed the trout with his dip net, it was full daylight. Sea gulls flew around the boat. Hal could see their pink eyes when they peered greedily at G:andpa's trout.

It was Scotty's turn to row, Rex's turn to fish with Grandpa. Grandpa told them just how to trade places without falling overboard.

Scotty weighed more than Rex. Hal found it was easier to row with Scotty. Sweep—dip—pull. Sweep —dip—pull.

Suddenly Hal said, "I see something running on shore."

"A deer, maybe," Grandpa answered. He turned to look when Hal pointed. Grandpa's eyes were old. He saw nothing unusual.

Rex looked, too. He said, "It's a dog. I think it's Hero."

"Put your glasses back on," Grandpa said with a chuckle. "That beach is a couple of miles from the cottage."

"Well, it *looks* like Hero," Rex insisted.

The boat was now headed toward the beach where Rex saw the dog. Sometimes the dog paused to look at the boat. Then it ran again.

As the boys turned in a big circle to return to the opposite point, Hal burst out, "That *is* Hero. See him run!"

Rex, Scotty, and Grandpa turned when Hal pointed. It was Hero, all right. Hero was running on the wet, hard-packed sand where the lake touched the beach.

Anxiously Hal said, "He'll get too hot."

Grandpa moved uneasily. He said, "Hero will have sense enough to cool off before he starts home."

But Hero did not turn back. He plunged into the lake. Straight toward the boat he swam, his nose lifted well out of the water.

Grandpa had a nibble. While he played his fish, the boys kept their eyes on the spaniel.

"Hero isn't getting any closer," Scotty said worriedly.

"Don't worry," Grandpa said. "Hero knows how far he can swim. He will go back to shore."

"Grandpa," Hal insisted, "Hero didn't go back, and I don't see him."

"Sure 'nough?" Grandpa asked. Crisply he ordered, "Stand up, Rex, and have a look. I'll balance you."

Rex took off his thick glasses. He looked long and hard at the shore. Then he said, "I see Hero. He is splashing, but he isn't moving ahead. He is in the seaweed."

"Oh, oh!" Grandpa said. Quickly he reeled in his long line. "Lift your oars, boys," he ordered. "I'll use the motor."

The outboard sputtered, then thumped with a busy *putt-putt*. Quickly Grandpa guided the boat

74

to the shallow water where the seaweed grew.

And there was Hero!

His collar was caught on a sunken pine bough. Tangled seaweed wrapped his legs. Only Hero's eyes and nose were above water by the time Grandpa leaned over the boat to set him free.

Gently Grandpa heaved the tired dog aboard. Hero shook till water flew. Then he lay on the floorboards. He put his nose on his front paws. Tired though he was, his tail thumped. Coaxing sounds came from his throat.

Grandpa smoothed Hero's wet fur. With a grin he said, "It's like I said. Boys, boats, fishhooks, and dogs don't mix. But, Hero, when you run two miles, then try to swim a lake to join us, we'll put away the fishhooks."

When Grandpa started the motor and headed toward the cottage, Scotty said, "Grandpa, Hal didn't have his turn at fishing."

"Who cares?" Hal asked. "We saved Hero's life. A live dog is better than a dead fish."

"Yeah," said Rex and Scotty.

Hero licked Hal's hands.

WHAT IS IT?

Hal sat on his heels. Katie looked over his shoulder. Both studied a track in the sand. It was a large track, clearly outlined at the edge of the beach.

"Would Grandpa fool us?" Katie asked. "You could make that print by tying some sticks together and pushing down into the sand."

"Maybe," Hal answered. "But we'd better find out for sure. Let's go."

Deer trails and watering places are the newspapers of a forest. To be safe in the woods it is necessary to know what has been where you stand. It might return.

At the spring this morning Grandpa had assigned tracks to be followed. When he went back to the cottage he had said, "Bring me some proof that you know what you're following. I'm taking nobody camping unless he can read trail signs."

Camping! Oh! Hal wanted that camping trip so much he could taste the wanting.

Rex, Scotty, and Polly had gone up the trail toward the deserted schoolhouse on the County Road. Hal was sure they were following a fat old porcupine. But this track in the sand—mmm. Hal had never seen one like it.

Katie moved away. She stooped low to study the ground. After a few minutes she called, "Here's a clear track."

Hal ran across the sand to see what she had found. Impatiently he said, "You're going backward, Katie. You're headed for the spring. Those toes point away from the spring."

With much dignity Katie said, "Well, at least I found one."

"And I didn't, huh?" Hal asked hotly. Without another glance at Katie, he walked in circles. He moved away from the spring while staying close to the lake. At last he found a single print. The toes pointed toward the marsh.

At this point no cottages were in sight. The beach was littered with all the trash washed up by storms. Huge rocks were tangled into the uncovered roots of great pines. Bushes grew thickly on the hillside.

Here the water of the bay was shallow. Overgrown with weeds and cattails, there was more mud than water. Tall grass grew on little islands. Water lilies floated in pools. There were clumps of buttercups and forget-me-nots. Turtles sunned here. Frogs ate mosquitoes.

Katie followed Hal. But she kept a sharp lookout for anything that moved.

"The track goes right into the marsh," Hal said.

"Mud squishes," Katie said, trying not to sound afraid.

"We'll use wood for stepping blocks," Hal said.

Together Hal and Katie gathered sticks of driftwood and large pieces of bark. Their trail led to deep mud covered with moss. Hal showed Katie how to drop the wood, make a bark platform, step, and make another. Then he picked up the pieces from the rear and built another stepping block. They crossed safely, but slowly. When they reached dry sand again, their arms and legs were caked with mud.

"What *are* we following, Hal?" Katie asked anxiously. "It's something big, I know. And it likes water."

"A rhinoceros, maybe?" Hal teased.

"It stands on one leg most of the time," Katie said.

"Or with one leg out of the water, and the other in," Hal said.

"I think it eats fish," Katie declared. "Animals don't just walk along looking at the scenery."

Suddenly Hal snapped his fingers. He grinned. "Come on, Katie," he said. "When you know what something eats, you know where to find it."

Hal set off down-shore, Katie following, half

running to keep up with Hal's fast pace. "Do you know what it is?" she panted.

"I think so," he said.

"A beaver, maybe?" Katie asked.

"There's no tail mark. Besides, a beaver doesn't stand on one leg."

They left the marsh. They followed the lakeshore under the cliffs which threw the echo. They climbed over a rocky point. When they reached a little bay, they faced Grandpa's cottage. It was shadowy here, filled with morning's coolness.

Silently Hal pointed.

At the edge of the beach where the water met the sand stood a great blue heron.

Katie gasped, "A bird! As tall as Scotty!"

"Isn't he something?" Hal asked softly.

The heron stood on one long, thin leg. It took a giant step without a splash. Only its soft blue and gray feathers and head plume moved. With its long, yellow bill the heron scooped up a fish. The long, long neck stretched to swallow.

Katie tried to move closer for a better view. She slipped on a pebble. The small sound startled the

heron. The great bird flapped into the sky. It dangled
long bare legs and feet. One blue feather floated
downward.

When the feather landed on the water, Hal stuck
it into one of Katie's heavy braids. "There now,"
he said, grinning. "You can prove we tracked the
heron."

"Do we have to cross the marsh again?" Katie
asked anxiously.

"Up on the hillside there's a game trail we can follow," Hal told her.

Barefoot, Hal led the way across the beach. He stubbed a toe and hopped for a minute, ouch-ing with pain. He picked up the small stone he had kicked out of the hard wet sand. Then he forgot about his toe. "Oh-h," he breathed. "An arrowhead."

"Let me see!" Katie demanded eagerly.

Together Hal and Katie looked at trees, rocks, and shadows. At some unknown time an Indian had shot that arrow.

Silently Hal put on his sneakers. He led the way up the game trail. Katie had a heron's feather to show Grandpa. But Hal had found something more important.

On some yesterday an Indian had tracked his game and shot his arrow. Today Katie and Hal had followed the great blue heron to its fishing spot. And tomorrow?

Tomorrow Hal wanted to walk on unknown trails, unafraid because he knew what had been there before him.

84

INDIANS

After Hal found the arrowhead, he talked about nothing but camping and Indians. Soon Scotty refused to go past the parking lot alone. Katie ran from her own shadow. Slowpoke Polly no longer took her nap in the hammock.

Finally Rex, the quiet cousin, asked, "Just where are those Indians, Hal?"

The three boys were shooting marbles in the backyard. Scotty put his taw in his pocket and stood up. He demanded, "Yeah, show us one!"

"They—I—" Hal stammered.

Helplessly Hal waved at the mountains behind the foothills. Back there somewhere men dug for gold, silver, and lead. Men cut down forests. Men hunted and fished. And there were Indians. Hal had seen them.

The Indians rode spotted horses. They herded sheep and worked on their own ranches. They worked in mills, owned businesses, and went to offices every day. They did not shoot stone arrows or ride the rapids of the big rivers in skin boats as they once had. But Indians there still were.

"Just what I thought," Rex said as Hal's silence lengthened. "There aren't any Indians!"

At just that moment Grandpa came down the path. He waved a letter. "We have an invitation," he said. "I suppose you wouldn't be interested in visiting an Indian camp."

"Indians?" Rex and Scotty repeated.

"Wow!" Hal shouted.

"This is from my old friend, Simon Tallman. He

is on his way to a rodeo where the young men of his tribe will ride," Grandpa explained. "They will camp up on Tepee Creek while the tribe gathers. They would like to see us."

Simon was a tribal leader. His sons had served in the armed forces with Hal's father and uncles. Simon owned a leather-goods shop. Members of his family made moccasins, saddles, belts, and purses. When the rodeo season came, they closed shop. They put on feathers and beads and rode in competition with western cowboys.

"Now you'll see an Indian!" Hal told Rex and Scotty.

Two days later Grandpa, Grandma, and the five cousins loaded the station wagon with picnic supplies. They headed north toward Tepee Creek.

The Gales ate lunch in a ghost town on the shores of a lake. Once it had been a booming mining camp.

While they ate, a band of sheep pushed down the street. A boy not much older than Hal guarded the "woolies." His only companion was a small black dog. The sheep climbed the steps of an old hotel. The boy rattled rusty tin cans on a loop of

88

wire. The dog herded the stray sheep back into the herd.

"That dog is almost as smart as Hero," Hal said.

"Sure," Rex said. "But where are the Indians?"

Grandpa's eyes twinkled. "That boy was not Chinese," he told Rex.

"Was *he* an Indian?" Rex asked in amazement.

Grandpa drove up and over mountains and across creeks. They passed several small bands of riders on horses. The animals were spotted like merry-go-round horses.

"Are those horses real Appaloosas?" Scotty asked excitedly.

"Are those men Indians?" Rex gasped.

"Yep," Grandpa said.

In late afternoon Grandpa drove into a long valley cut through towering stone mountains. He parked in a meadow filled with cars, pup tents, trailers, and wickiups. Several decorated tepees stood in the tall grass.

In a cleared space a noisy game of baseball was going on. A tall man left the ball game. He saluted as he came toward Grandpa.

"Hello, there, Simon!" Grandpa shouted.

"Howdy, howdy," the man shouted back. He wore a plaid shirt tucked into Levi's. His black hair hung in two long braids. He wore a high-crowned black hat.

Behind his thick glasses Rex's eyes missed nothing. He saw that the older men were dressed much like Simon Tallman. Sun glistened on the young men's butch haircuts.

The older women bound their hair with silk scarves. They clutched fringed shawls around their shoulders. Sleeves and skirts were long. Moccasins were boot-high and tightly laced. Teen-agers wore shorts.

When nobody was looking, Rex pinched his own arm to be sure these Indians were real. They were.

Grandpa's friend, Mr. Tallman, led the Gales to the ball field. A wrinkled woman shared her bench with Grandma. Sturdy children welcomed the five cousins.

One boy ran to a cooking fire. He brought back hot dogs, popcorn, and pop. While he passed the food to Rex, Scotty, Katie, Polly, and Hal, he yelled, "Kill him, kill him!" Then he muttered with good-natured disgust, "That umpire is nuts!"

After the ball game, there were races for the children and wrestling for the men. One group of men sat under a tree to play a "stick" game. They did not look up when the young men raced their spotted horses around and around the clearing. The wild kiyi-ing shouts made the hair prickle on the back of Hal's neck.

When it grew dark, a huge bonfire was lighted. People disappeared briefly, then came back. They wore fringe and feathers, fur and beads. Faces were painted. Great headdresses bobbed. Red and yellow, purple, green, and blue colors glowed in the firelight.

Drummers sat in a circle. Drums began to throb. An old woman shrieked. She held a long, high note till the cousins moved uneasily. Then she began a chant.

Men and boys leaped into the cleared space around the fire. Bending and rising, stamping and turning, each danced alone. Fast—faster! When excitement seemed to reach a peak, the drums beat

faster and the dancers kept step.

On a blanketed throne sat an ancient chief. His great headdress was made of eagle feathers. A fat baby wearing a white diaper toddled among the dancers. He stamped his feet and waved his arms.

"They'll step on the baby!" Katie cried.

But they didn't, and the dance ended as suddenly as it had started.

Then men, women, and children moved into a circle. Shoulder to shoulder, they began a silent step —step—slide circle dance.

Members of Simon Tallman's family pulled the Gale cousins into the circle. Rex danced on one side of a boy with bells on his ankles. Hal danced on the other side.

When Hal swallowed the lump in his throat, he saw that Grandma and Grandpa were dancing, too. Grandma wore a purple shawl. Grandpa's white hair was bound with an orange handkerchief.

When the drums stopped beating, Hal nudged Rex. "Are you having fun?" Hal asked.

Rex pushed up the thick glasses he wore. "Oh, boy!" he cried. "Indians!"

95

HAL, THE BEAR SLAPPER

Grandpa's cottage stood apart from the summer colony on Blue Lake. Perched on the cliff, the house faced the lake. Its back was to the forest. On its left, a creek flowed down from the mountains. On its right, marsh spread from the spring in a deep ravine. From the beach to the County Road, the Gale cousins played where they chose.

Grandpa protected the cousins from danger. Every morning he walked with them to see what animals had come for water during the night. They went up the lane, down the marsh path, and around the lower trail. They walked down deer trails and pushed through bushes.

Soon Hal, Rex, and Scotty learned to spot the tracks of the small animals: skunks, porcupines, squirrels, chipmunks, rabbits, gophers, and field mice. Several times they noticed a doglike track. Then they saw a coyote on the ridge above the creek. At night they heard his queer, gargling cry.

Even Polly and Katie knew the sharp prints left by deer. These tracks might be found in sand, mud, or in the woods.

On the shore they found the wiggly tracks of water snakes and turtles. They were no longer confused about the prints of the heron, the bird as tall as Scotty.

But one track puzzled them. Grandpa was not with them when they found it. They were playing wood tag on the hillside between the lane and the spring.

Rex found the track near the spring. He squatted on his heels to look at it. Then he called Hal. "What is it?" Rex asked.

Hal did not know, but he guessed. "A big porcu-pine, maybe?"

At just that moment Scotty charged down the hillside. Both Rex and Hal raced to find a cedar, the "safe" wood today. Cedars were hard to find. Scotty caught Rex. The boys forgot to mention the track when Grandma called them to lunch.

The next day Hal found the same print near Grandpa's station wagon in the parking lot. Polly had spilled a bag of potato chips when the cousins helped Grandpa carry groceries to the cottage. Every bite of the salty food was eaten during the night. In the hot dust the prints were fuzzy. Then Scotty stepped in the clearest one.

Rex scowled at Scotty. He did not call Grandpa to look at the print. "No use, when it's all messed up," he grumbled.

That night they heard a bawling sound. The boys lay on their cots on the sleeping porch. They tried to figure out how a calf might have reached the beach. They went to sleep with the mystery un-solved.

The next morning they found a row of tracks on

100

the beach. Rex and Hal were sure they matched the others they had found.

Rex said, "Hal, keep your eye on Scotty while I go for Grandpa."

Scotty shrugged and grinned. He sat in the sand with his arms around his knees. Polly and Katie sat with him.

When Rex brought Grandpa to the beach, Grandpa had only to glance at the tracks. He said, "I wondered how long it would take you to find that bear cub's tracks."

"A b-bear?" Polly stammered.

The five cousins looked at each other in dismay. They remembered the bear which had kept them up in the trees in the orchard.

"Does this mean we can't go out of the yard to play?" Hal asked.

"No," Grandpa said. "It means you must use your eyes and ears."

"And nose," Scotty added. Scotty noticed odors. He remembered the musty smell of the old farmhouse.

Polly went back to the cottage with Grandpa.

After a while Katie followed.

The three boys marked lines in the sand to practice broad jumping. They did not play in the woods that day or the next.

But after a while they forgot about the bear cub. There were not enough hours in the day to do all the things they wanted to do.

The boys wanted to sleep in the woods. "We need practice for our camping trip," Hal said. But they did not have nerve enough to put their sleeping bags on the ground.

"I don't want a deer to step on me," Rex said.

"Or a bear," Scotty added.

Because of the "age in his bones" they did not ask Grandpa to sleep with them.

"We need a tree house," Hal decided.

Rex, Scotty, and Hal searched the hillside. They needed four trees which grew at the four corners of a small square. Also, the trees must be large enough to hold up a platform.

After much looking and measuring, they chose a spot above the spring.

"I don't know," Scotty said slowly. "Some of those

animals that go for water at night can climb trees."

Hal asked Scotty, "Who's afraid of a porcupine?"

Rex agreed with Hal. Finally Scotty gave in. They began their search for pole-sized young trees. Grandpa allowed them to chop young trees growing too close together. "Just be sure you leave no trash in the woods," he said.

They cut the limbs from a dozen young trees. They used pine boughs for sleds. Then they dragged the trash on the boughs to the beach. There it dried for a bonfire.

They wanted their platform ten feet above the ground. Scotty tried to drag Grandpa's stepladder through the woods. He gave up when it hung on bushes along the way.

Rex finally thought of nailing sticks to the "corner" trees. Then they climbed the tree trunks like walking up a ladder. It was not easy to balance, since the tree-ladders were straight up and down.

Hal tied a piece of rope around himself and the tree trunk. He planted his feet solidly on one of the sticks. He leaned back against the loop of rope and worked with both hands.

105

After this the work went faster. They crisscrossed poles to make their platform.

Rex squinted through his thick glasses. "It isn't exactly level," he said.

Cheerfully Hal said, "We'll sleep with our heads uphill."

"Sure," Scotty agreed. "If I fall out of bed, I want to land on my feet. I might want to run!"

Long before dark they carried three sleeping bags and air mattresses to their tree house. They tied a long rope around a bedroll or mattress. Then

one boy climbed the ladder with the rope in one hand. Hand over hand he drew his supplies through the air like drawing water from a well.

A dozen times during supper they asked Grandpa, "Are you sure it isn't going to rain tonight?"

Each time Grandpa said, "No, it won't rain."

Grandma suggested that they undress in the cottage. "Wear your pajamas over the hill to the tree house. Then you'll only have to worry about losing socks and sneakers," she said.

Scotty was slow about brushing his teeth and getting ready for bed. It was almost dark by the time the boys went to the living room to tell Grandpa and Grandma good night.

"Shall I walk with you?" Grandpa asked.

Each boy wanted to say Yes. Bravely they said, "We'll be all right, Grandpa."

"Be careful," Grandma warned. From their cots Polly and Katie echoed, "Yes, be careful."

"Take Hero with you," Grandma called.

The light was almost gone when the boys left the backyard. By the time they entered the deer trail which led past their tree house, the cousins were

three pale ghosts walking through shadows. Each boy hesitated to be first to switch on his flashlight. So they hurried along, through the growing darkness, not saying a word.

Hal was leader. Down the trail trotted a small animal. "Go faster, or get out of the way, Hero!" Hal ordered. He slapped the animal's rump. With a grunt and a "Woof!" the animal trotted faster.

"H-Hal!" Scotty stammered, from the end of the line. "If you slapped Hero, wh-what is following *me?*"

Instantly three lights clicked on. To Hal's astonishment, he found himself trotting at the heels of a fat bear cub!

"I-I-I—" Hal gasped through chattering teeth. "I slapped a bear, and he didn't slap back!"

Pell-mell, Hal, Rex, and Scotty rushed to their tree house and climbed to their beds. As they zipped their sleeping bags, Hal asked, "Are you afraid, Scotty?"

"No," Scotty said. "Hero is under our platform."

"Why should we be afraid?" Rex said. "We're sleeping with old Hal, the bear slapper!"

109

A DOG WITH SENSE

"Which way shall we go, boy?" Grandpa asked.

Hal jumped into the air. When he landed his toes pointed north. That is the way they took.

Grandpa walked with his knees bent. He said that eased the stiffness in his joints.

Hal raced up, down, and across the County Road. He left tracks in the hot dust.

Dozens of times Hero dashed into the woods.

110

But he always came back to dog-laugh at Hal and Grandpa.

Once they heard Hero bark in the valley. That is where the creek ran. Later his bark echoed from the rocks along the lakeshore. Then they heard Hero high on the hill.

"He's up at the farm now," Hal told Grandpa. "Maybe Hero is chasing a bear."

"That dog!" Grandpa said, chuckling. "He would bark up a storm at a grasshopper. He wants me to follow him. He has no respect for the age in my bones."

"He's a good dog, Grandpa," Hal said quickly. When Hal was in the woods he liked to know that Hero was near. When they camped in August, Hal certainly wanted Grandpa to include Hero. But only good dogs are useful in the wilderness.

"Hero is a good pet," Grandpa said. Then he sighed. "Maybe he's just too young to have sense."

"Hero has sense. He knows lots of tricks!" Hal insisted. "Hero can roll over, sit up, speak, say his prayers, and—"

Grandpa laughed aloud. He held up one hand.

"Okay, okay, boy," he chuckled. "But Hero does tricks for a pat on the head. That doesn't prove he has common sense. Now, boy, I had a dog once—"

"You mean Jerry?" Hal asked.

"Yes," Grandpa said. "There was a dog with sense. He knew the names of each person in the family. He carried notes. He ran errands. Jerry used his head."

Grandpa whistled softly, remembering his dog, Jerry.

While Grandpa walked and thought, Hal whooped for Hero. Hero bounced out of the woods. He ran circles around Hal.

This was the kind of day Hal liked best. The sun was hot. Grasshoppers rose each time he took a step.

"Catch some of those 'hoppers, boy," Grandpa said. "We'll feed the trout in the creek."

"I'll catch if you'll carry," Hal said.

"I'll carry," Grandpa agreed. He cupped his big hands to make a tight, round house. His right thumb was the door. When Hal poked in a grass-hopper, Grandpa shut his thumb-door.

112

"Don't lose them, Grandpa," Hal warned.

The creek ran through a cement pipe under the
County Road. A cool forest trail went up one bank
of the creek. Grandpa, Hal, and Hero left the road.
They walked up the deer trail. It was so quiet, Hal
could hear Hero pant.

They came to the first of the deep pools. Brook
trout swam there.

"Now?" Grandpa asked. He wiggled thick, white eyebrows.

"Now," Hal agreed.

Grandpa moved his thumb. A grasshopper poked its head through the opening. Hal caught the grasshopper. He tossed the 'hopper far out into the pool. Grandpa chuckled when a trout flashed to the surface. Hero bounced and barked.

Further upstream the creek dropped over rocks in a little waterfall. This pool was deeper than the first. Hal saw a fish dart from under a tree root when he threw a grasshopper. He tried to catch the trout with his hands and almost fell into the pool. "Someday I'll catch one," he declared.

"I'd try, if I didn't have age in my bones," Grandpa said. "Cold water sets my joints to aching."

One by one Grandpa and Hal fed the grasshoppers to the trout. Finally Grandpa had just one grasshopper left. He said, "I think I'll walk out on that log. I'll see if I can coax a whale out of the shadows."

A fallen tree made a narrow bridge across the deep pool. Carefully Grandpa stepped out onto the

114

log. He grunted when he bent his knees. Hal heard his knee bones creak.

"Be careful, Grandpa," he warned.

"I'm always careful," Grandpa said cheerfully. "I—"

C-r-r-rack!

Grandpa was heavy. The log was very dry. A long split opened in the dead wood. Grandpa teetered. He tottered. His feet danced. He tried to turn on the log before it came apart.

Grandpa turned. He waved his arms for balance. Just as the log fell into the water, Grandpa landed on shore. "I m-made it," he panted.

"But your hat didn't," Hal told him. "There it goes."

Grandpa's straw hat floated in the pool like Noah's ark, its brim flattened out like a deck.

Grandpa rubbed the fringe of white hair around his bald spot.

"I'll get your hat," Hal offered. "Cold water makes your bones hurt."

"You'd better not try, boy," Grandpa advised. "That creek is snow water right off the peak. You're

116

hot. You could get a muscle cramp."

"Then I'll wade when your hat floats out of the pool," Hal said.

"We'll forget about my hat. You'd sink in swamp mud."

"You mustn't sunburn your head, Grandpa," Hal said worriedly. "You could wear my hat—"

"If you hadn't left it home," Grandpa reminded.

"Oh, that's right."

Silently Hal and Grandpa watched the straw hat turn in a little whirlpool. Hero dangled his red tongue. He watched, too.

Hal looked at Hero. Cold water did not bother Hero. Nor did Hero mind the mud. Suddenly Hal remembered Grandpa's dog, Jerry, the dog with common sense. Well, maybe Hero had common sense, too.

"Fetch!" Hal ordered.

Hero was always ready to play. He waggled his tail. He flipped long ears. His bright eyes peered at Hal's hand, waiting.

"Fetch, Hero!" Hal ordered again. He waved and pointed at Grandpa's hat.

Hero wiggled with excitement.

"F-E-T-C-H!" Hal shouted.

"Boy, I told you Hero just knows a bag of tricks," Grandpa said. "He is waiting for you to throw something for him to fetch."

Hal threw a piece of pine bark. It landed close to Grandpa's hat. By the time Hero swam after the bark, the hat moved. Hero brought back the bark.

Grandpa grinned at Hal. Then he rubbed Hero's ears.

"When Hero sees that hat, he will bring it back," Hal insisted.

Grandpa winked. He teased, "To train a dog, you must know more than he does."

By this time Hal felt he had to prove Hero had common sense! But, how? That hat was moving on the current. When Hero swam, the water moved. Then the hat moved faster. Besides, Hero kept his eyes on the stick that was tossed.

But—what if the stick sank?

Oh! Hal had an idea. He grinned at Grandpa, then looked for a flat, thin stone. He found one just made for "skipping."

Hal swallowed before he said, "I think so."

Two hours ago Grandpa had said, "You may hike for one hour. Then eat your lunch and come home."

The hour had passed. Lunch was eaten. Now, which deer trail led back to the cottage? All the trails looked alike!

Many trails led into this clearing. Beaten-down grass and hundreds of small hoofprints showed this to be the bedding ground of a herd of deer.

Hal knew they must be at the top of the foothill on which Grandpa's cottage stood. All trails led downward.

Hal knew, too, that a few of those trails would lead downward only a little way. Then they would climb up and up into the dense forest of a huge mountain. He must not lead these city children into the wilderness.

The first time Hal had seen Rex, the boy from New York City had said, "When we get off a sidewalk, we're lost." Well, they were off a sidewalk. And they were lost. A shiver ran down Hal's spine.

Rex said, "We've learned to track animals. We

should be able to track ourselves."

"Sure," Scotty agreed. "We can look for tracks in the dust."

"What dust?" Katie asked. She pointed at the hard-packed earth. Brown, dry pine needles covered the ground.

"I wish we hadn't played hide-and-seek," Polly said mournfully.

"We'll have to look for other signs," Hal said. Soberly the five cousins scattered, looking for

small, telltale signs among the trees and bushes.

Katie did not like cobwebs in her face. When she walked she waved a stick like a baton. Sometimes she struck a bush. This left bruised leaves to wilt.

Polly tore petals from flowers while she walked or hid during a game. On three trails they found goldenrod petals.

Scotty kicked stones like a football. Little holes showed where stones had lain.

Signs were found on many trails. Not even Hal could decide which trail they had used to enter the clearing.

"I wish I'd stayed home!" Polly wailed.

125

Hal wished so, too, but he dared not admit it.

At the end of one of these trails Grandpa and Grandma were probably sitting in the front yard. Grandpa would be reading. Each time the shade moved, he would move his chair. After a while he would tilt his chair against the front wall of the cottage.

With a deep feeling of loneliness Hal looked at the patches of shadow at the bases of pines. Then he shouted, "Shadows!"

Rex looked puzzled, but interested.

"At Grandpa's cottage the shadows point uphill in the afternoon, away from the lake," Hal explained. "To go back to the lake, we must walk into the shadows, not away from them."

"Oh, sure," Rex agreed.

The five cousins rushed into the first trail they found where the shadows of pines pointed at their feet. They walked fast, then faster, not even using breath to talk.

Polly was youngest and plumpest. After a while she panted, "I'm t-tired."

"Me, too," Katie said.

126

They stopped to rest beside a great stone.

Suddenly Hal realized he had never seen that stone. They had not come this way. But, how could he tell his cousins?

Hal did not have to tell them. Polly, Katie, Rex, and Scotty turned from the stone. They looked up-trail and down-trail. Then they looked at each other with blank faces. The eyes in each face were large and dark with fright.

Before Polly cried, Hal looked at the shadows. "We're going toward the lake," he said. "When we get to a beach, we'll figure out where we are."

"Oh, sure," Rex said. "There are cottages all around the lake. Somebody will take us home."

The next time they rested, Katie said, "We should be able to see the lake by this time."

"We walked for an hour before lunch," Rex reminded her.

Katie argued, "But that was uphill!"

Silently Hal agreed with Katie. By this time they should be able to see Blue Lake. Instead, Hal saw pines, firs, cedars, birches, cottonwoods, maples— Hal drew in his breath. Maples and cottonwoods

127

grew near water, that he knew.

But, what water?

While the girls rested, Hal looked for a rock to climb. When he stood on top of a great stone, he no longer wondered where he was. He knew.

This trail led into the swamp.

The swamp spread from the creek where he had fed the trout with Grandpa. Beavers had crisscrossed logs to build many dams. A deep, wild jungle of woods, water, and mud filled the whole valley. The swamp reached from Blue Lake to some far-away spring on a mountainside.

Silently Hal climbed down the rock. When he faced his cousins, he said, "We'll see which way the water runs. Then we'll know which way is downhill. We'll walk down to the lake."

The first sign of danger was found around the next curve. The remains of a deer lay in the trail. A great claw was fastened in the hide. Rex picked it up. Slowly he said, "Sometimes our cat loses one of his claws when he scratches the stair rug."

The cousins huddled close together. No house cat had killed that deer. A cougar had used this trail!

"I wish we had brought Hero!" Polly wailed.

"Do we have to stand here?" Scotty asked. "That cat might come back."

Slowly and quietly the cousins went down the narrow path. In a very few minutes they reached the end of the game trail. Ahead lay mud and water. With so much underbrush it was hard to see the sky. The marsh was deeply shadowed.

Hal tossed a twig into the water. He knew it would float downhill, toward Blue Lake.

The cousins held their breath till the twig began to move. When the twig began to float, they walked in that direction.

There was no game trail to follow. The cousins went under bushes, over logs, around stones, and through mud. Sometimes they waded through murky water.

Often they found themselves trapped in a tangle of mud and brush with no way to go ahead. Then they crawled out to try again and again until they found a way to move forward.

When even Hal had decided they were completely lost, they crawled under the branches of some young cedars.

And there was Blue Lake!

Sun warmed the beach. Light sparkled on the tops of small waves.

"Now we're not lost," Polly said.

"Not lost!" echoed Katie, Rex, Scotty, and Hal.

Hal thought he had never heard such wonderful words. Not lost!

SWAMP TRAIL

After finding their way back to Blue Lake, the five Gale cousins ran across the beach. They splashed water over muddy arms, legs, and faces. Polly hummed. Katie sang. Scotty shouted.

Hal shook his wet hands till water drops flew. Then he frowned. Something was wrong. What was it?

Scotty yelled again.

Then Hal knew what was wrong. No echo repeated Scotty's words!

Hal looked at the empty beach. Then he saw that no boat docks rocked on the waves. No paths led to cottages. No cottages perched on a cliff.

And, *where* was the cliff?

Polly stopped humming. She asked, "Are we still lost, Hal?"

"I—don't—know," Hal said honestly.

"This *is* Blue Lake, isn't it?" Katie asked.

Rex took off his glasses. He pointed at a white line on the opposite shore. He said, "I see a cliff, and Grandpa's house."

Katie pulled one of her braids. She almost whispered, "We're on the wrong side of the swamp."

"Are we, Hal?" Polly asked.

Hal nodded.

"How did we get here?" Scotty asked.

"Before we got to that clearing, we crossed a creek twice," Hal said. "We thought it was the same one, but it wasn't. We must have crossed the swamp creek above the beaver dams."

"Then we didn't come down the hill behind Grandpa's house," Rex said thoughtfully.

"No. We came down the hill next to it," Hal said.

Polly wailed, "We *are* still lost!"

"No," Hal told Polly. "We aren't lost. We are on

134

water and swam slowly away.

Hal took a step or two. Then he looked back. To his surprise, he saw that the spot where he had seen the beaver was the end of a trail and that trail led into the swamp itself.

Hal waited until Rex, Polly, Katie, and Scotty stood beside him. Then he showed them the trail. He said, "If this trail crosses the swamp, I can lead the way home. I've been as far as the third pool with Grandpa."

Rex rubbed one foot on the earth. "This trail looks dry," he said.

"Do you expect us to *crawl* through the swamp?" Katie asked.

"I'm s-scared!" Polly wailed.

"So am I," Hal admitted.

Katie winked back tears. "Let's vote," she said.

Hal asked, "How many want to go back to the clearing and hunt for the trail to Grandpa's cottage?"

Katie pulled a braid. She said, "We might not find the clearing. The swamp trail is right here."

The five cousins voted to try and follow the trail,

if possible, to the other side of the swamp.

"I'll lead," Hal said.

"Then I'll go last," Rex said.

Hal looked at his city cousin with respect. There was as much danger at the end of the line as at the head.

"Ready?" Hal asked soberly. "When we start, we must keep going, no matter what happens."

"Ready," said Katie, Scotty, Polly, and Rex.

Hal curled his fingers into fists. Then he dropped to his knees and entered the beaver trail.

For many yards the children crawled through a cool, dim tunnel. The earth was hard packed and clean, but filled with the musty odor of wild animals, fish, and rotting logs. Strange rustlings could be heard. Once something splashed. An animal squealed, whether in anger or in pain, Hal could not tell.

Hal reached a spot where a great, mossy log blocked the trail.

Was this the end? Would they have to back out?

Cautiously he stood up. Then he saw that the trail led across a small island. When a deer stamped

141

a warning, Hal knew it was possible to walk to shore. That deer was too large to crawl through the tunnel. The deer whistled through its nostrils. It stamped again. Then Hal saw a fawn drop to the ground behind a bush.

As the children hurried across the island, a kingfisher screamed. The bird dived for a fish. A marsh hawk's wide wings spread shadows on the ground. A great blue heron flapped into the air. It sailed out over the swamp, dangling long legs.

The cousins found deep water at the edge of the island. Hoofprints showed that deer leaped or swam. The children crossed on a mossy log.

Again they crawled, not saying a word nor knowing what they might meet. One thing they knew: A cornered animal would fight.

At last they reached the end of the swamp trail. With a long, trembling breath, Hal stood up and looked around. "We made it," he told Polly, who had followed him the whole dangerous way.

Gladly the five children trotted down the hard beaten trail to Blue Lake.

They had gone a very short distance when something caught Hal's attention. Had something moved? Or had his ears warned of danger? He did not know.

One by one the cousins crowded past Hal. They hurried on down the trail. Hal shrugged and thought, "I'm getting jumpy." Then he looked up.

His muscles seemed to turn to ice. On a branch directly above the trail lay a wildcat! Slanted eyes looked down at Hal. A tail twitched.

Polly, Katie, Rex, and Scotty had passed under this same bough. The cougar had not harmed them.

But—they had not looked into the cat's eyes.

Warily Hal studied the animal. Then he saw that the hips were not raised into position to spring.

Hal took one soundless step. Then another and another. He shivered with fear when he passed under the bough, but he knew he must keep walking.

A dozen steps away from the cat, Hal glanced back. The cat had not moved. Its eyes followed his every movement.

Hal let out his breath with a sighing sob when he reached a curve in the trail. He was safely past the cat.

"What's the matter?" Rex asked when Hal caught

up to him. "Did something happen back there?"

"There was a cat," Hal whispered. "Don't scare the girls and Scotty."

An hour later the children met Grandpa in the lane above the parking lot.

"Grandpa!" they shouted gladly.

Tears filled Hal's eyes. In his whole life he had never been so glad to see Grandpa.

"What happened?" Grandpa asked. "I've searched for hours."

"You didn't search the swamp," Hal said soberly.

"The—swamp?" Grandpa repeated in alarm.

While they walked down the lane, the tired children told about being lost and facing danger. When Hal told about the cat, Grandpa's arm went across his shoulder.

"You're ready for that wilderness camping trip," Grandpa said proudly.

Hal forgot about fear and tiredness. Eagerly he asked, "When do we go?"

"Next week," Grandpa promised.

Unable to say a word, Hal looked at Grandpa and grinned till his cheeks wiggled.

CAMPING!

All summer Hal had worked for the chance to camp in the wilderness with Grandpa. At last Grandpa had promised, "Next week, boy." And this was "next week!"

Deep in the heart of a national forest Grandpa set up camp beside a creek which drained ice water from the mountain peaks. Each morning when the sky turned pink the five Gale cousins crawled from sleeping bags. There were never enough hours in the day for all the things they wanted to do.

148

Katie had packed a large book in case she became bored. She had no time to read. Each night she pressed wild flowers and leaves between the pages of her book.

Rex found a tiny gold nugget in a crack in a rock. He spent many hours searching for another.

When Scotty became hungry, he sat among huckleberry bushes and ate till his mouth turned purple.

Polly ran camp errands for Grandpa. She whistled at the marmots in the rockslides above the creek.

Hal found an agate when he helped Rex hunt for gold. On the peak of the tallest mountain he found bear grass for Katie, and picked up an eagle feather for Polly. He gathered big, juicy blackberries from vines growing in the rockslide. Hal saved half the berries for Scotty. With Grandpa, Hal found the meadow where the mule deer bedded at night and discovered where the eagle nested.

Most of all Hal liked to fish for trout. Rex and Scotty dangled their lines from rocks along the creek bank. Hal waded right down the middle of the stream.

They were fishing at sunset on the fifth day when

Rex shouted, "I'm cold. I'm going back to camp."

"Me, too," Scotty echoed.

Down at the bend of the creek Hal could see Grandpa's campfire. Polly and Katie moved from station wagon to tent to campfire while they helped Grandpa cook supper. Hungrily, Hal wondered what they were cooking. Then his trout fly disappeared under a rock ledge. He forgot about food while he fought to land the trout.

While he worked, Hal whistled between his teeth. Hero answered the whistle. The dog scrambled over the great, smooth stones to watch Hal. Hero dog-laughed and made little talking sounds.

When Hal landed the trout, he shouted, "Got him, Grandpa!"

"Bring him in, boy," Grandpa called back. "I'll clean that fellow and fry him for your supper."

While Hero leaped over stones on shore, Hal waded the swift, shallow water. Scotty met Hal and carried the trout to Grandpa.

"I can't quit while the trout are biting," Hal told Scotty.

By the time Hal snagged a second trout, he was

close enough to camp to smell a fish sizzling in
bacon fat. With a shout of laughter, he heaved the
fish from the water and swung it to shore, still dangling from his line. Rex took it from Hal's hook.
Rex tossed the trout to Grandpa, who promptly
cleaned it for the frying pan.

"Keep 'em coming, boy," Grandpa called.

Hal had been aware of small night sounds—an
owl's cry, wind in pine needles, the click of a deer's
hoof on stone. But suddenly there was another
sound. Hero growled.

Hal jerked his head to see what had disturbed
Grandpa's dog. Every hair on Hero's body bristled
like the quills of a porcupine. Hero's lips pulled back

153

from his teeth, but he was not dog-laughing. Hero stared past Hal to a log which made a bridge halfway across the creek.

And there, so close he could almost reach out and touch it, stood the biggest, blackest bear Hal had ever seen outside a zoo!

With a frightened gasp, Hal stepped backward. He almost lost his balance. The small splash he made attracted the bear's attention. It lowered its head. It squinted through small, nearsighted eyes.

Just a few yards down-creek, Grandpa and the cousins laughed and talked around a campfire. But here in the fading light Hal faced three hundred pounds of danger. Hal tried to shout, but no sound came from his tight throat. He drew a shivering breath and stared back at the bear.

The bear shifted weight. It grunted with annoyance, then slapped the water. For an endless second Hal waited for the slash of sharp claws. Then Hal saw the flash of a dripping trout in the bear's paw.

While the bear ate the trout, Hal eased backward, step by step, till he reached dry ground. Then, with

155

Hero leading, he rushed to the safety of Grandpa's campfire.

Grandpa chuckled and pointed at Hal's hand. He asked, "Did you snag one you couldn't land, boy?"

To Hal's amazement, he discovered he still carried his fishing rod, but the line was tangled among rocks and bushes along the creek.

Hal heard a thud in the gathering dark. When the bear had disappeared, he answered shakily, "No, Grandpa. But he didn't snag me, either."

Katie served the food. Polly passed the plates. Rex talked about the black sand he had seen. "Betcha there's gold someplace close," he said eagerly. Between bites, Scotty fed Hero from his plate. Grandpa added a log to the fire and mused, "Now, I had a dog once—"

"Was his name Jerry?" Hal prompted. Hal smoothed Hero's ears while he listened to Grandpa's story. Someday, when Polly and Katie were not around to get scared, Hal would tell Grandpa about the bear on the log.

Happily, Hal thought to himself, "I've LIVED an ADVENTURE."